The Tupilak

Written by
Kathryn White

Illustrated by Diana Mayo

CHAPTER ONE
THE CURSE

Quenna clutched the ivory carving tightly in her mitten. 'Why, oh why did she have to find the Tupilak?' she asked herself helplessly.

At first she had thought it beautiful, strangely beguiling. Its ivory face was perfect in detail, and its tiny intricate eyes seemed to draw her, beckon her to pick it up.

Like a magnetic force, irresistible, it had waited for centuries, lying dormant deep in the ice, its secrets ready to be re-awakened.

Once she had succumbed to its power, touched the cold ivory, it seemed that it was not she who possessed the object, but the object that possessed her.

Quenna stared out across the white sea of snow, pondering the safest route.

'There,' she thought. Her eyes tracked along the line of the massive blue oil pipeline that stretched its ugly coils far out into the distance.

'If I follow the pipe, I won't get lost. It will always lead me back to the village,' she thought reassuringly to herself.

She looked anxiously down at the Tupilak.

'Quenna, keep me,' it seemed to whisper to her in the breeze. 'We belong together ...'

Quenna shivered.

The snow sparkled like diamonds, reflecting its pureness and beauty back at her. This was reality. Not the world of myths and legends, of fantasy and fear that had always engulfed her grandmother and those from an age before her.

Quenna loved jumping the ice with friends, paddling in the kayak, breathing in the fresh Alaskan air. These were the things that made the world, her world.

She looked down at the strange carved face and felt renewed, determined. 'You must become a myth again,' she said softly.

She strode out, occasionally glancing back at her village, reluctant to take on the journey that she should have made weeks ago. The further she walked, the less she looked over her shoulder, as each time the sounds of barking dogs, radios and life's general mayhem became more distant, muffled. After a while all she could hear was herself, padding gently in her kamiks on the crisp, hard, shimmering snow.

She tightened her grip on the ivory carving in her mitten. She had to send the carving back to where it had come from. She would dig deep down into the ice and return it to her ancestors – only this time it had to stay there, frozen in time forever.

The Tupilak had changed her life. It had had a terrible effect on her and her family.

Too many dark events had happened since she discovered the Tupilak to think they were coincidence. She knew it had to be the power of the evil Tupilak at work.

Her grandmother said she had felt its strange, evil influences as soon as it was brought into the house, but the family had mocked her superstition.

Now, as Quenna walked, listening to her breath and feeling its warmth as it rebounded from inside her hood, she realised that on that first day they were already trapped in the darkness of the Tupilak.

Their mockery of their elder, her grandmother, was real and painful. The Tupilak's power was already exerting itself, tearing the family apart. They just didn't see it.

Before the Tupilak, life had been

wonderful. She was like her peers, an Inupiaq child; happy with her past, respecting the history of her elders and excited by the future.

Her father once cheerfully travelled to the oil plant; he earned well and was happy with his independence. They had money, a nice big log cabin with enough rooms for all, good food, warmth, and television – so much more than many others in their village.

Her mother helped with the school and community affairs, and her elder brother Ituku would be leaving school soon.

Lastly, she thought of her grandmother and suddenly felt overwhelmed with sadness.

Her grandmother had once been so happy. Her face was always set in a wide, cheerful grin. Her dark eyes creased into smiling lines. When she laughed, it was such a deep and infectious laugh that soon Quenna and the whole village could not resist laughing too.

Her grandmother's strong yellow teeth would gnaw tenaciously at the small chunks of sealskin and her hands, wrinkled yet as transparent as cloud, would adeptly stitch the skins into beautiful mittens and kamiks.

Sometimes she would pull Quenna into her arms and hug her as tight as a polar bear, roaring and growling playfully until Quenna wriggled free and won the game.

That was before the Tupilak.

Tears welled up in Quenna's dark almond-shaped eyes and began streaming down her cheeks. The cold air bit at her wet, reddened skin. She lifted her small mitten and carelessly wiped her face. Her mitten skin hardened crisp as the wetness of her tears turned to ice.

She, Quenna, had brought home the Tupilak and with it, the curse. On that day her grandmother had descended into a strange kind of madness. Fear overwhelmed the old woman like a disease, and nobody had cared.

Quenna's anger rose. She lifted the Tupilak up to her face, resolute in her decision to be rid of it. This battle she would win!

CHAPTER TWO
THE SPIRIT OF NANUQ

Quenna clearly remembered where she had found the Tupilak. It was the day she had gone out with her father checking the route for the annual sled race.

She figured it to be about half a day's walk from the village and, as she had set off on her journey so early in the morning, she would return home without the Tupilak long before darkness. Her short dark plaits bounced on her shoulders as she stamped on; faster and faster, harder and harder her feet struck the smooth white ground.

Quenna remembered the look of horror on her grandmother's face when she had proudly held out the Tupilak for her to see.

'Where did you find that evil thing?' her grandmother had asked in horror.

'On the journey back, Grandmother. It was deep down in the ice, but I chiselled and worked and dug it out. Look, there's not a scratch on it, it's perfect.'

'Quenna, it holds great power. It is very, very old, see? The face is evil! It is a Tupilak.

Cast it away, little one, before it harms us all,' her grandmother had pleaded.

'What rubbish,' Quenna's mother Saufak said dismissively. 'Sometimes your grandmother still lives in the past with the stories she spun out to me when I was little. Keep it. It is very old and made of ivory. It is our heritage, we must respect it.'

'Fools,' said her grandmother. 'Saufak, when did you stop listening to your elders?'

'When my elders started to speak rubbish,' Saufak replied.

Quenna's mother took the carving from Quenna and held it up. 'Look, Mother, it is a toy, no more than that.'

'It is an evil Tupilak,' Quenna's grandmother insisted.

Saufak sighed. 'It is ivory, carved into a beautiful image. How can anyone think this object evil?' she said, puzzled.

'I have seen the powers of the Tupilak at work,' Quenna's grandmother said, frightened. 'Only a Tupilak carved from greater magic will protect us.'

'Hey, Quenna, better get carving,' Ituku said, throwing his empty cola bottle at her.

Quenna caught it playfully. 'I'll carve it in your image,' she said, 'that's bound to frighten the demons.'

'Mock your grandmother, Ituku, but who was it that rescued you from the floating ice when you were younger?' snapped her grandmother.

Ituku shrugged reluctantly. 'You, Grandmother,' he said quietly.

'Mmm.' Her grandmother frowned. 'Perhaps if your father had taught you more about ice than about playing with engines, you would not have wandered into danger.'

Saufak handed the Tupilak back to Quenna. 'It is time to leave these myths behind,' she said sharply to her mother.

'Time does not change the power of the Tupilak,' her grandmother said darkly. 'The demons become stronger.'

Quenna shivered.

'Enough talk of evil demons, they are children's fairy tales,' Saufak said angrily. 'The only demons in this house are the bills we have to pay.'

So came the first crack in their happy family unit.

Quenna's grandmother sat worrying in the corner of the kitchen. She rarely spoke to Quenna but watched from darkened eyes as the power of the Tupilak took hold.

There were nights when Quenna listened to the sound of her grandmother chanting in the darkness as if in prayer, and shadows danced across the snow outside.

'Your grandmother is being a fool, and the moon and cloud are playing tricks with your eyes,' Quenna's father told her when she spoke of it, but his voice was impatient.

It seemed as if their big log cabin was shrinking. The presence of her grandmother's fear caused anger and tension between everyone.

Now Quenna realised that if only she had listened to her grandmother's wisdom, Theo her dog would still be alive.

Quenna remembered that horrific morning as if it were yesterday.

She had opened the cabin door and stepped out into bright sunshine. The night storms had subsided and the snow had already hardened like rock.

Quenna picked up the bag of seal bone and plodded across the yard to where Theo and the other husky pups were housed. Things seemed strangely quiet and she knew instinctively that something was wrong.

Normally Theo barked and scratched at the wooden barrier, eager to get to her for affection and food, but today all was still.

As Quenna approached, she saw the pen smashed down on one side and splintered wood littering the yard. The husky pack was huddled together, silent, terrified under the wooden cover.

Quenna pulled them out, counting one by one, her eyes searching desperately for her beautiful dog – but Theo had gone.

Quenna started to call his name, then she saw the blood.

Small dots at first, bright scarlet, splattered on the hard white snow inside the pen, but the trail grew deep and dark, disappearing into the small back-lands of discarded oil drums and old machinery.

Quenna followed the trail.

She lifted the dirty drums and shoved them from one side to another, calling for Theo. He had gone, vanished, and all that was left were large, strange animal prints.

'What's going on?' her father said irritably, hurrying out of the cabin.

'It's Theo, somebody's stolen Theo,' Quenna said, distraught.

'Quenna, this is a small community. We all know and trust one another. No-one would steal Theo,' Saufak said calmly.

'But it's true. He's gone, look.' Quenna pointed to the broken pen.

Just then her grandmother appeared.

'Nanuq!' she shouted as she knelt on the snow. 'It is Nanuq the evil spirit bear who has stolen Theo. See what your curse has brought to the village,' she said accusingly to Quenna as everyone gathered around.

Her father bent down and ran his fingers across the marked snow. 'They do look like polar bear tracks. If this bear has left the wild it will be a great danger to everyone in the village. We have no choice but to track it.'

'You will never find it now,' said her grandmother. 'It is an evil spirit, and guns cannot destroy the spirits.' She dug her fingers deep into Quenna's arm and shook her. 'You must throw away the Tupilak. All this is your doing, you foolish child. It is your fault that this has happened. Now you have drawn an evil Nanuq spirit to the village.'

Quenna shook with anger. 'I loved Theo. He was my favourite dog. I wouldn't do anything to harm him,' she cried out. 'You're horrible to say that. I will never throw the Tupilak away now, never, never, never!'

It was the first time that Quenna's grandmother had ever physically hurt her. They had always been so close.

'Stop this foolishness or we will no longer speak to you, do you understand?' Quenna's father shouted angrily at her grandmother.

Her grandmother slowly stood up and, defeated, walked back into the cabin.

Quenna's father threw up his arms, exasperated yet remorseful at his outburst.

'She complains that I do not teach my son to hunt, and when I speak of hunting she speaks of evil spirits,' he said angrily.

Saufak frowned. 'Mother has seen many changes in her life, we must not forget that.'

'But the changes are good,' said Ituku, thinking of his skidoo snow-scooter.

'Not all change is good, son,' his father said darkly, 'not all.'

Quenna's father and Ituku reluctantly prepared their sled and, once ready, the huskies pulled them away on their search for the polar bear.

Quenna and Saufak went to the kitchen. Grandmother was sitting at the table, her hands quickly flicking a needle in and out of the skin linings. She looked up at Quenna, her dark eyes full of anger and resentment.

Saufak sighed impatiently. 'Come on, there is work to be done at the community centre,' she said to Quenna.

As Saufak frog-marched Quenna across the village, Quenna looked sadly back at their log cabin. The thought of her grandmother sitting in the kitchen, lonely and isolated, made her churn and twist inside.

'It is best not to feed your grandmother's fears,' Saufak said, catching Quenna's anxious glance. 'We must be strong.'

Quenna drew in a deep breath and walked on in her silent white world. The blue pipeline seemed to grow fatter, stretching out its gigantic body, casting shadows over Quenna and the snow around her.

She realised that was the first battle the Tupilak had won, but there were to be more.

It seemed hard to believe that her favourite pup had been stolen by a polar bear. It was the first time in nearly 20 years that a bear had ventured into the village. Over the years, the machinery, radios and noisy snow-scooters had deterred the mighty beasts from coming in too close, but something had drawn Nanuq to them. Perhaps the beast was so starved that it didn't care about the risks it was taking by facing man.

Or perhaps it was the dark power of the Tupilak.

CHAPTER THREE
THE ENCOUNTER

Quenna's legs were beginning to ache.

She knelt down and gouged out a small hollow in the snow. She pulled a piece of sealskin from her pocket, unfolded it and carefully laid it down. Then she sat on it, nestling comfortably into the hollow.

She dug deep into her fleecy pocket and took out a bar of chocolate. She placed the Tupilak on the ground in front of her and slowly chewed on the chocolate bar.

All the while she kept a watchful eye on the Tupilak, as if it were a wild creature about to flee and she would have to chase after it.

She looked up above her head straight into the underbelly of the blue pipeline. It was giant and unyielding, spreading its mass above her and across the white land. She imagined the thick black fluid pulsing through the pipe, poisonous, burning up the beautiful white snow, throwing its oily slush into the seas.

She had found some oil once, sloshing up onto the icy shore. It seemed to be so beautiful. When the oil mixed with the sea it had created a rainbow effect, lavenders and yellows, blues and pinks. But when she had put her hand in the water the oil had drawn itself apart, slippery and alive, covering her skin like a disease.

The more she had tried to rub it off, the more it spread across her flesh. Her grandmother spent hours painfully scrubbing the oil from Quenna's arms until all that was left was bright red, burnt skin.

Her grandmother tutted and complained about the filthy black slime.

'That slime pays me well and keeps us fed and warm,' said Quenna's father.

'If you hunted, we would not need the slime,' her grandmother said.

'We no longer need to hunt to survive,' her father replied with relief.

'Just as well,' Saufak said, winking, 'or we would all starve to death.'

Her grandmother shrugged in disgust as she battled with oil scum clinging around the sink.

That was Quenna's first encounter with oil, the precious oil that the world seemed to love, but she knew that the thick, black, shiny fluid was deadly, and was always wary of it.

Quenna's brother Ituku, on the other hand, loved the oil now. He poured the black stuff into the motor of his skidoo snow-scooter and tore around the village. Pop, pop, went the engine as he shot over the snow, veering this way and that, racing wildly with his friends.

Her grandmother had looked on with delight and relief when the motor on Ituku's skidoo had burnt out and peace temporarily returned to the village.

'Ah, you see, Grandson, huskies never break down. You can always depend upon the nature of the dog.'

'Don't worry, Gran, I'll have the skidoo fixed in no time, then you can come for a ride with me,' he grinned cheekily.

'Huh!!' Grandmother snorted with disapproval.

Often Ituku accompanied his father to the refinery, and when they returned Ituku, smiling with glee, carried in great packs of snacks and fizzy cola.

'And when will you teach your son to hunt?' her grandmother had asked her father.

'When the oil runs dry, Mother, when the oil runs dry,' her father said.

'His teeth will rot,' her grandmother stated flatly.

Saufak took the snack packs from Ituku's arms. 'Mother, these smell nicer than raw seal meat, try them,' she said.

Quenna's grandmother put her hand to
her nose in disgust. 'Pickled onion, huh,
never, never,' she said with contempt.

Quenna giggled, then devoured two
snack packs in one go.

When the chocolate was finished Quenna
stood up, picked up her sealskin piece and

placed it back into her pocket.

She bent down and swept the Tupilak back up into her mitten. She reckoned another two hours' walk would bring her to where she had discovered it.

Quenna remembered the sled trip with her father and the thirteen huskies that had taken them there.

They were a quick pack. The leader was a beautiful white and gold husky, and was intelligent and instinctively a leader. He was also Theo's father.

Theo was the most beautiful puppy Quenna had ever had.

Sometimes when her parents were out, Quenna's grandmother would turn a blind eye to Theo and Quenna playing in the kitchen.

Often Quenna was caught by her father and admonished, and Theo was sentenced to the harshness of the pen outside.

'It is important for us to have good relationships with our dogs,' Quenna's grandmother told her one day as Quenna played with Theo in the kitchen. 'They are hardy, but if we are kind to them, they are loyal and more obedient.'

Quenna touched the fur around her hood and thought of Theo's soft warm body, and as she looked ahead she suddenly spotted a tiny object walking aimlessly across the snow.

At first she couldn't make it out, but as it drew closer she was certain it was a dog – either a very small one or perhaps a young puppy.

It trotted across the snow and then stopped suddenly, sniffing at the ground.

Quenna screwed up her eyes, desperately trying to bring the creature into focus. As it moved across the white horizon it would stop every so often, look around, then hurry on.

Quenna waited and watched it coming towards her.

As the animal came into focus it bore a strange resemblance to Theo. Its main body was white but its lower back and tail seemed to be a beautiful golden colour.

Theo had had such unique markings, there was no other dog like him.

Quenna's heart missed a beat and her face flushed hot with excitement. She had finally found her Theo!

The creature came to a halt and sat a short distance off, as if obediently waiting for her.

Quenna started jogging quickly towards it. 'Theo,' she called excitedly as she approached the animal. Now she was only metres away, and as the animal came into view Quenna staggered to a halt.

The dark brown eyes of an Arctic fox looked coldly at her. It didn't move; it just sat glued to the ice, staring strangely.

Quenna's heart sank.

The fox was in half change for the winter. Its brown fur had turned a brilliant white over its head and main body but left a golden dark covering over its back and tail.

It was as beautiful as Theo, but a dark wildness glinted in its sharp eyes.

Quenna and the fox stood only feet apart, locked in visual combat.

The fox was as still as the air around it, almost merging into the snow. Its gaze was empty, uncaring, blank.

Quenna's grip tightened around the Tupilak. 'I hate you,' she whispered in the wind. 'You have played a cruel trick on me.'

She felt covered in an invisible blanket of darkness as the curse drew over her. Angrily

she reached down into her pocket and took
out the small sealskin patch. She rolled it
into a tight ball and threw it with all her
might at the fox.

'Go on, get out of here, evil spirit.'

The sealskin slapped onto the fox's side
and fell to the ground. The fox snarled. Its
black eyes flashed amber, then it turned and
trotted off as if it had never been touched.

Quenna stormed up and retrieved
her sealskin. Shaking with anger and
disappointment she rammed the skin into
her pocket. She looked back along the blue
pipeline, fighting back the tears. She wanted

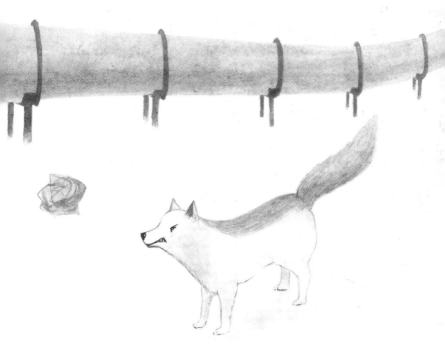

to turn back, desperate for comfort from her grandmother.

When she turned around, the fox had disappeared. Her eyes searched the open snow for even a tiny speck of the animal, but it had vanished.

Fear began to well up inside her. Would the magic of the Tupilak be too much for her to resist? The magic wasn't even something she could touch. At least if she could see it she could fight against it, like the whale.

Yes, the whale.

How could she forget that day?

CHAPTER FOUR
SEA OF BLOOD

Quenna had set off in her kayak, one of six small boats paddling in the harbour.

Her friends shouted they were going to race back to the dock, but in the end it had not been a race with her friends but a race against death.

Quenna had decided to let her friends win – she was in no hurry. It was a day to lap up the sunshine and fresh breezes. She dipped her paddle into the water and turned her light, small kayak towards the dock.

Her friends were way ahead, and once they docked, they shouted in triumph across to her as she paddled idly along. She watched them dancing on the wooden platform, honking and doing seal impressions. Suddenly their shouts changed and became urgent, frightened. They jumped up and down, waving frantically at her.

'Lunatics,' Quenna thought. 'The times they try to trick me.' She smiled to herself, waved back, and kept paddling gently along.

But suddenly the waves around her changed and became choppy.

Then she saw the fin. Off to her left, it seared through the water like a knife through lard. It was black, jagged, torn at the top and heading in her direction. As soon as she saw the flash of white, Quenna knew it was a killer whale – a young one, but still many times the size of her tiny kayak – and it was coming straight for her! Her heart raced.

'Help!' she yelled out as she hammered her paddle with all her strength, down into the deep. Suddenly the water felt like sludge, heavy, thick and impossible to move.

Then her kayak lurched and catapulted forward.

The whale had come up under her kayak and its back had skimmed the base of the boat, carrying her forward for many metres.

The kayak jarred to a halt and bounced erratically on the choppy surface.

Desperately Quenna clenched the wooden paddle in her fists and hit out frantically at the end of the whale's fin but it had no effect on a beast of such size. The whale flipped to one side, covering her kayak with icy-cold water as it vanished into the depths.

Quenna sat in silent terror. She watched the froth bubbling, changing directions, as the water was churned up beneath her in the depths. The whale was coming in to circle her kayak again.

'Help, help!' Quenna screamed. She struggled frantically to escape but the kayak skins seemed to be alive – as if clinging to her body and keeping her locked in, trapped for the killer whale. Then she heard the distant sound of a motor. A small fishing boat was ploughing towards her.

Men stood out on deck, shouting instructions to her, but she couldn't hear, and she couldn't move. She was frozen in terror, waiting for the beast to strike.

The whale surfaced far off to her left and swam full on at her.

Her mind raced; she couldn't understand its behaviour. Never before had she heard or seen such a thing as this. It must have thought her kayak was a seal and was toying with its prey.

As its great black and white body careered toward her, Quenna desperately lashed out at it with her paddle.

It turned, and its large powerful body swept up into the side of her boat.

Quenna went rigid.

The lashing waves became magnified in her head as the force of the impact swept her along sideways for what seemed a lifetime.

She was rolling a high wave up over the whale's massive body. The beast was carrying her along, taking her down to her death.

She felt her tiny kayak lift high into the air, then it tipped over as if in slow motion. Gently her kayak toppled and turned like the twist of a screw and her face slapped down hard onto the ice-cold water. She shuddered as the water stung at her cheeks and enveloped her head.

Now the kayak was floating upside down. Its fragile base bounced on the water's surface. Bubbles appeared, encircling the upturned vessel as trapped air popped to the top. Quenna hung helplessly upside-down under the blue rippling water, caught in the upper skins of her kayak. She could see the light of the sun on the surface from underneath.

She heard a distant, muffled growl growing closer, second by second.

'What's happening?' she thought in terror, as the growling grew deeper and deeper and the water vibrated and shook around her.

'Remember.' Voices rang out in her head. 'Remember, Quenna, how your father taught you to turn your kayak.'

In terror, Quenna clutched her paddle tightly with bony white knuckles. She moved her paddle under the surface, silently in a

strange world. She tried rocking from side
to side, as her father had shown her. She
began pulling her body one way, then
allowing it to fall the other, building up the
momentum she needed to twist back up and
re-surface, but she was stiff with terror and
her movements were awkward and slow.

Quenna choked inwardly, but resisted
swallowing the painfully cold water. Her
eyes, round and white with fear, searched
the moving blue mass expecting the killer
whale to appear before she could re-surface.

If it hit her, it would be the end.

Suddenly the water changed from blue to a deep mauve. 'Uhh, no, no!' her mind screamed. Terror wrapped around her as her watery world transformed.

Now the growl was so close she could almost feel it touch her skin.

Quenna braced herself, waiting for the black mass of the whale to open its mighty jaws and rip her from the kayak.

Suddenly she found herself the right way up. She surfaced into harsh daylight. Coughing and spluttering, her lungs dragged in the cold air.

The fishing boat was bobbing beside her kayak, its motor rumbling gently in the water.

Quenna looked into the face of Noah, one of the village fishermen. He had been lowered down beside her kayak and managed to reach across and pull it upright.

The other fishermen were shouting and calling to one another. They reached down and pulled her heavy, cold body from under the kayak skins.

As Quenna was lifted up alongside the fishing boat, she caught sight of the dead whale.

Its massive body was floating just below the surface of the water with a harpoon in its side. The waters around it were dark and murky with blood.

Once they knew Quenna was safe, the fishermen prayed for the release of the spirit of the killer whale to be reborn into another generation.

When they reached land, Noah drove Quenna home on his skidoo and proudly carried her back in to the safety of her cabin.

When she heard of Quenna's terrible ordeal her grandmother said, 'Hear me, Quenna. It is the curse of the Tupilak.'

Quenna recovered quickly and had a moment of happiness when she had searched through her pockets and discovered the Tupilak missing.

'It's gone!' she thought triumphantly. 'It must have sunk to the depths. I'm free.'

But Noah had carefully checked Quenna's kayak and had found the Tupilak at the bottom of the kayak. Later that evening, he appeared with a happy smile and handed her the Tupilak as if he had saved not only her life but a great treasure for her too.

Quenna was so relieved to be alive that she thanked Noah and took the Tupilak back into her possession.

It had won again.

Quenna turned from her tracks and faced the wilderness ahead. Yes, she thought, the Tupilak has great power.

She drew in a deep breath. 'But this time I will not give in.'

Quenna walked on, faster and faster. The light of the sun began to cut through her dark mood and cheer her spirit. As she marched on she pulled from her pocket a band of string and wrapped it around her fingers.

Quenna made an ajarraaq. Cleverly she looped one end over a finger and drew it across her hand, making a shape by looping it across her other fingers. 'Fish, fish, in the dish,' she sang to herself. Making string puzzles cheered her up.

Quenna unwound the string and made another shape. 'Star, star, near and far.'

Time and again she cleverly shaped the string into different objects.

It was her favourite game at school along with Piklirtautiniq, where she could jump from kneeling straight up and onto her feet faster than anyone else. 'Quenna, the queen of Piklirtautiniq,' her friends called her.

Quenna smiled inwardly and carried on with her string game. 'Baby in a crib, feed it squid,' she sang. Again the string unwound, but this time it fell to the ground. She reached down to pick it up, but it had fallen into a shape on the snow.

Quenna could see the shape clearly. She went down on her haunches and ran her fingers along the outline.

It was a whale.

Quenna shivered as she remembered her ordeal. Gingerly she picked up the string and put it in her pocket.

The Tupilak had again drawn another nightmare from Quenna's mind.

'I won't let you win,' she said softly.

CHAPTER FIVE
THE ICE PALACE

The soft breeze was turning to a sharp wind that danced about Quenna's cold face and flapped her fur hood.

The silence unnerved her. She felt her solitude magnified in the empty whiteness.

A shadow passed over her and, looking up, she saw a skein of snow geese sweeping across the sky, their cries reaching far out into the wilderness. The geese looked chaotic, happy, normal.

It was sights such as this that made Quenna feel safer, calmer, and helped her in her battle against the sinister forces of the Tupilak.

Quenna's confidence began to grow.

She wondered what her family would be doing now.

Her father would be lying on the sofa bed, as he had been since the accident, frustrated and in pain. He would open another can of beer and drink himself to sleep to try to forget.

Quenna tried to block the memory, but it flooded into her head.

She could still smell the hot foods baking out in the village street, smell the smoked fish hanging, mouth-watering, above her head.

She could see the happy, expectant faces just before the sled race.

Mushers prepared their sleds, alert, ready to start.

Her father waved over at her from his sled, then squatted down to check the dogs, making sure the ties were loose enough yet secure enough to pull his weight.

The build-up to the race was full of fun. It brought out the whole village, laughing, challenging, waiting in anticipation for the competition.

Quenna's favourite event was the blanket toss. She climbed up onto the caribou skin and the whole village gripped the blanket edges tightly. Then up, up, up into the air they tossed her, higher than the roofs. She'd come down and bounce onto the soft skin, then flick, up she'd fly again, looking out into the world.

Each child had to spot the target from the high toss. Quenna never did. She loved the toss so much that she never bothered pretending to look. She just allowed herself to fly and twist and bounce in the air for as long as she could.

This was Saufak's happiest time too. She'd prepare the village hall, looking proudly at the banners she had made for all the events. The community centre doors were flung wide open and there was food and drink for all.

Quenna's grandmother sat in a special area set aside for the elders. She drank and ate and talked with her friends about the old exciting races and friends that had passed through time.

Then everyone gathered around the competitors.

Huskies barked and howled in excited expectation.

Mushers stood tensely, bracing themselves, ready for the signal.

Then they were off.

Quenna's father was third in line as sled after sled sped away amidst barking dogs and shouts of glee.

Brown, slushy snow shot out from under the sled rails, covering the spectators as they shrieked and waved at mushers shooting past.

Later that night, Quenna remembered the sky. It was aglow with lavender and red, yellow and gold; a myriad of shooting lights, flashing and changing colour.

Her grandmother had told her it was the gods racing across the sky, chasing the caribou with golden bows and arrows.

Her mother tutted impatiently and told Quenna it was the northern lights, the aurora borealis, caused by particles from the sun interacting with the Earth's magnetic field.

Quenna found both explanations interesting, but much preferred imagining the gods teaming across the sky in their magical sleds in pursuit of caribou.

Her father had been so close to the end of the race when he'd hit something. Something so massive, it scattered wreckage over the whole width of the racing line.

The rest of the mushers had to speedily re-route their packs. This was a nearly impossible task – normally there was no need even to direct the sleds.

The dogs knew the route; it had been programmed into their minds since they were young.

The race lasted for eight hours, and when the riders returned they were exhausted and triumphant.

This year it had been different.

Her father couldn't remember what happened. Whatever it was, something was there waiting, and when they impacted it was like an explosion. The sled shot off the ground and spun into the air. By the time the sled made its last roll across the ground it was carnage.

Huskies wandered dazed and confused, and her father lay in agony with broken bones under the remains of the shattered sled.

It had never happened before.

Her father had always been careful and checked the route. That was what they were doing out together on the day she had found the Tupilak.

Yes; the Tupilak, Quenna thought. It had to be returned now or she might never have the chance to do it again.

Quenna stopped and leaned against the mighty blue standpipe. She clenched the Tupilak tightly. She felt a strange darkness descending. What had happened to the sunshine? Suddenly, heavy grey and lavender clouds were being drawn from all directions, converging above her in a floating mass. Quenna speeded up, panting nervously inside her deep fur hood.

Far off in the distance she was relieved to see the first signs of closing in on her destination.

Tall ice caverns and glaciers reached up majestically from the snow.

When she had first seen it with her father it had taken her breath away.

Ice mountains shot up in mighty towers of sparkling white that glinted in the fiery sun. Birds perched all along the ridges, as if guarding a secret haven.

Quenna had dreamed about living in an ice palace, and here she had found it. She had first spotted it in the distance and, although it was not on the sled route, she

had begged her father to take her there.

Her father had laughed at her fantasy and said it was beautiful, but every year great chunks of the ice and snow broke off, toppling and crumbling to the ground.

'Soon, after standing for centuries, your very own ice palace will have melted away. But for now, it is one giant of an igloo.' He chuckled as the sled swept through the caverns.

Quenna looked up at the white towers. The howling dogs cried out inside the mighty structure and echoes reverberated all along their route.

'Only something magical, beautiful could live in a place like this,' she said to herself.

It seemed too perfect for any human, herself included, and so she felt she had to reluctantly hand her beautiful ice palace over to a goddess. Yes, she thought, this is the home of some wonderful, kind goddess.

For just beyond the beautiful ice structure was the site where she had found the mysterious Tupilak.

CHAPTER SIX
FINDING MAGIC

Quenna remembered the first moment she saw the Tupilak.

Her father had stopped at the side of the ice palace to rest the huskies and Quenna had stepped from the sled and wandered as usual. Her short, sharp steps had taken her some distance from the sled.

She glanced back and her father waved reassuringly to her. Then she looked down at her feet. Her kamiks stood either side of an object set in the ice.

Quenna pulled out her sealskin piece and knelt down beside it. She rubbed the light snow covering from the surface of the ice as if it were dust, and blew gently.

The Tupilak looked teasingly up at her, its fine carved lines lightly blurred by its depth in the ice, but she could clearly see its yellowy form.

Quenna stood up and raced back to her father's sled.

'I know you're bored, Quenna, we'll be off in a little while,' her father said in anticipation of her moans.

'No, please don't go yet, I've found a hidden treasure,' Quenna said, jumping with excitement. 'Please, please just let me try to dig it out,' she pleaded.

Her father sighed with exasperation and handed her a small pouch of tools from the sled. 'Lose them and you will pay for new with your own money,' he told her flatly.

Quenna's face lit up. She grabbed the tool kit and flew back to where the skin lay on the ground. She took out the hammer and an assortment of tools and selected the best for the task. Then she started to chip hard at the ice. Carving out the ice around the Tupilak, she made a perfect square. Down, down she gently tapped the pick, inch by inch, second by second.

Quenna chipped patiently away, cutting out a neat square block to lever out. Her warm breath steamed up from the ice square as she drew close in to it, concentrating hard on delicately retrieving her treasure.

Suddenly she felt a hand on her shoulder. She looked up at her father, and pointing at the ice block, asked for his help.

He crouched down beside her and rubbed his hand over the square. 'Ha,' he said proudly, 'you will be a great igloo maker.'

Quenna's eyes sparkled with delight as her father took the pick and cleverly eased out the ice block. He held it up and looked intently at the carved object inside.

'Mmm, what do you suppose a child's toy is doing out here in the middle of nowhere? I think maybe there was a camp here long ago. It looks very old,' he said, intrigued.

'I told you it was a treasure,' Quenna said triumphantly.

Her father handed her the small ice block and laughed. 'I doubt you will get a tin of beans for that. Come on, time to go.'

Quenna placed the ice block carefully beside her on the sled.

They glided along the ice, Quenna's father shouting to his pack as Quenna perched on the fur skins like a queen. She remembered her excitement, as the sled thundered through the cavernous ice palace like a howling dragon. Quenna sensed the magic all around her. If only she had known that the magic she had felt was an evil Tupilak!

If only …

That night it seemed as if the whole world was on fire. But the real fire was still to come. The fire that had finally sent Quenna on her journey back to the site of her discovery.

On the night of the fire, Quenna had to believe that everything her grandmother had said about the Tupilak was true – if not for her own sake, then for her grandmother's.

Quenna had to believe in magic; one that has no boundaries but exists down through time as sure as the sun and the moon above. She had to believe in the power of the Tupilak.

Quenna could never be sure of anything again, and this was hard for her to accept.

Her father had taught her to read the world with her eyes, to hear it with her ears, to smell the changes in the air and sense the weather on her skin. Suddenly things happened not because of the power of the sea or the force of the winds but because of magical, invisible forces beyond her world.

The power of the Tupilak.

CHAPTER SEVEN
THE LESSON

It had taken Quenna's grandmother five long months to build up the wonderful hand-stitched collection of kamiks and mittens for the plane to collect.

Planes frequently flew in, but every six months a plane arrived with the task of delivering a quantity of fresh skins for the elder women to use their expertise in making traditional wear for sale to tourists and for export.

Quenna's grandmother was proud of her ability to create such wonderful things to sell and to contribute to the family funds. Her earnings were never high, but she felt her work made her worthwhile in the household and proud in the community.

Grandmother believed that she carried on a great tradition, and was desperate that it should not be lost to the cheap trashy mementos of the modern mass market.

Sometimes Saufak would hold up a new fleece or coat purchased from mail-order stores, and Quenna's grandmother would tug on the new fabric and tut and sigh with an expression of disgust.

'Saufak, you will freeze to death in that rubbish. You should wear caribou or seal.'

Saufak would look up to the heavens in exasperation. 'Nobody wears skins any more, Mother. These garments have beautiful designs and are tried and tested so that they are warmer than any skin.'

'Huh, if skins are good enough for the caribou and seal to survive in, then they're good enough for me. You won't see a polar bear wearing a blue floral fleece like that,' her grandmother announced.

Quenna howled with laughter at the thought of a polar bear in her mother's best blue jacket, but her mother was not amused.

Quenna's grandmother was always secretly sad that her daughter had stopped stitching the skins as soon as she was old enough to have a mind of her own and do other things.

'It is like you have become ashamed of your own people,' Quenna's grandmother said sadly to Saufak one day.

Saufak bristled as if a feeling of guilt had swept over her. 'What use is stitching, Mother? Our children will have to compete with people who have the power to press buttons and change everything around us. What are a few kamiks and mittens against the might of technology? I am only doing what I think is best for your grandchildren.'

'If you sever your ties with the past you will also make your children faceless and alien. They will not survive, even with your technology.'

'I can never please you, so I shall stop trying,' she replied bitterly.

So Quenna's grandmother took Quenna in hand and she began her training.

First she taught Quenna how to use the ulu, a sharp knife, to scrape the fat from the dead skin.

Quenna's father made a frame and her grandmother stretched the skins to dry them.

Quenna had many attempts at cutting the skins to pattern, but her grandmother became frustrated at her clumsiness. 'Look, Quenna, what shape is this?' she'd ask in dismay.

'It's for kamiks,' Quenna said innocently, believing her efforts were wonderful.

'Huh, it looks like polar bear droppings,' her grandmother said, disgusted. 'And what can you make from that? Nothing.'

Quenna giggled; her grandmother smiled and put her straight onto stitching.

This she enjoyed. After school, Quenna spent many happy hours stitching while her grandmother trimmed the skins and told her the wonderful legends of her people.

Quenna never noticed the time and her fingers soon became hardened to the needles and the strong threads.

Quenna began to feel the same pride and satisfaction her grandmother said she had felt on first completing a full pair of mittens and kamiks.

Saufak distanced herself from Quenna's pleasure and became more intent on

teaching Quenna what she could about technology.

She frequently battled against her mother by frog-marching Quenna over to the village community office where she instructed Quenna on how to use the computer. Quenna longed to escape the grey screen and return home to her grandmother's tales and stitching her wonderful mittens.

At the back of Quenna's cabin was a store room. It always smelt of skins and oil, and her grandmother's main task was keeping it warm and dry. All along the inside of the room were wooden slats, four layers in all.

When the plane took off, the store room shelves would be completely empty. All of Quenna's and her grandmother's hard work had been loaded onto the plane.

Her grandmother used to hug Quenna proudly and say, 'Think of all those people wearing our clothes, Quenna. Our work will spread all over the world.'

Then the store room would suddenly be filled with shapeless, heavy skins, waiting to be made into more beautiful clothing.

Her grandmother inspected each new shipment. Anything that didn't meet with her high standards was put to one side until the plane returned six months later. Then her grandmother would give the pilot a piece of her mind. 'Lady, it's not my fault. I'm just the postman,' the pilot said, throwing up his arms in dismay.

'Well, don't you post me rubbish again,' her grandmother chastised.

It was strange that on the night of the fire, Quenna was lying in bed looking at the Tupilak and had decided her father was right.

He had always said the Tupilak was just a chunk of cleverly carved ivory; it was old, but someone had carved its intricate face and design so carefully that he thought it would be wrong to discard it because of her grandmother's irrational fears.

'Keep it, Quenna, your grandmother will soon forget you've even got it,' he said reassuringly.

The yellow moonlight flooded in through her tiny bedroom window and the beautiful carved face seemed to glow up at her.

She tried to imagine the maker of the Tupilak. Never knowing that hundreds of years later Quenna would find it, chip it out of the ice and take it home almost as a gift from her.

Yes, Quenna thought, if I had learnt the skill of carving, I would have made a beautiful piece like this.

That thought pleased Quenna, and she began to value the Tupilak as her mother had said, as part of her heritage. She remembered holding the Tupilak in the moonlight; then she must have fallen asleep, because in the depths of the darkness she heard distant cries and shouts.

She opened her eyes and sat straight up.

The clock said 2.30 am.

Suddenly her bedroom door burst open and Ituku ran in.

He threw her kamiks and hooded qulittaq at her. 'Get up and out quickly, there's fire,' he said, then disappeared.

Quenna struggled up and threw her outer kit over her pyjamas. Now everything seemed urgent, frightening. It must be serious, she thought anxiously. She suddenly caught the smell of smoke drifting in from outside.

'Quenna, come now,' Saufak shouted.

Outside in the yard Quenna saw her grandmother yelling in distress. Her father was desperately trying to calm her.

The huskies had been taken out first.

They were yelping and barking in fear but had been tied for safety to a far-off tree.

Her father was struggling. He was hobbling on his crutches, angry and frustrated, as all he could do was shout instructions.

Ituku was tearing back and forth across the yard to the oil mound and scooping up massive empty drums of loose snow, then throwing it at the burning store room.

'Ituku, you fool, the drums have had oil in them, they will make it worse,' shouted Saufak angrily. She grabbed the shovel and started to frantically dig and throw snow at the flames.

All Quenna could see was fire.

Flames reached up to the sky as the fire roared on. The heat became so intense that everyone had to move back.

Suddenly their neighbour Tatigat arrived with his sons.

Now everyone was fighting to stop the flames from spreading to the log cabin.

While his sons swept across the yard dousing the store room, Tatigat banked up snow along the side of the cabin.

The heat was so close to Quenna's home that as soon as the snow was shovelled to the walls it melted away. Ituku and the other boys now had a good system going, and it soon seemed as if the fire was under control.

The red fire lit up the whole area, spreading its crackling, pungent smoke out into the dark wilderness.

After two hours of battling with the heat and flames, everyone stood scattered around the yard, feeling shocked and exhausted.

They had at least saved their cabin.

Black ash spread out across the white snowy yard in the shape of dirty boot-marks.

The store room had been completely destroyed.

Her mother emerged from the kitchen with trays of hot drinks for all, and everyone sat around drained and unhappy, talking quietly with Tatigat and his sons.

Relieved, Tatigat and his sons left.

Tired and miserable, they were about to go back into the cabin when Quenna's grandmother suddenly appeared at the cabin door.

Her grandmother was white with fear and shaking as she pointed her finger at Quenna. 'Quenna, this is all your fault. It was you who brought the curse of the Tupilak upon us. You!' she said angrily.

Quenna suddenly felt overwhelmed with guilt, and stood silent, upset and confused.

She was sad for her grandmother and sad for herself. Together they had worked so hard to make those lovely clothes and suddenly she felt responsible for all the loss.

Saufak stepped defensively in front of Quenna. 'You must stop it. Life is like this. We must accept good fortune and at times, the bad. You are teaching Quenna such stupid things,' she said angrily.

'Saufak, what do you know of these things? You stopped listening to your elders a long time ago,' her grandmother said.

Quenna's grandmother looked different, as she had never seen her before, cold and frightening. Even her voice sounded strange.

'You cannot blame a child for all our misfortunes,' Saufak said angrily.

'It is the Tupilak, I tell you,' her grandmother shouted.

Quenna's father dragged himself up and hobbled in pain over to the remains of the store room. He had seen something.

He balanced on one crutch and reached out for the object with the other. He lifted out a large black pot from the ash pile. It was still smouldering hot and smoking from the fire.

It was her grandmother's oil lamp.

He looked across at her grandmother and held it up by its hook. 'You left your oil lamp on,' he said flatly. 'It must have tipped over.' He discarded it angrily back onto the ash.

Her grandmother's eyes flashed in fear. 'Never, never once in all my time have I ever left an oil lamp unattended.'

'Well, this time you must have done,' Saufak said sharply. 'You are older. These things happen.'

'No! No! All my work is destroyed,' her grandmother shouted desperately, 'and you all blame me, when it is the Tupilak!' Distraught, her grandmother turned away and fled back to her room.

The rest of that night seemed to go on forever. Quenna sat alone on her bed in the sickly smoke-filled air, trying to block out her grandmother's sobs.

Quenna knew she had to do something she had resisted facing for weeks. At sunrise she dressed, took the Tupilak from under her pillow, and left silently, like a shadow.

CHAPTER EIGHT
THE ICE GODDESS

Quenna's heart soared. She had made it.

She stood under the beautiful ice palace and looked up at its magical white towers.

She breathed in the fresh snowy air and looked out on the other side of the structure.

There it was, the site where she had found the Tupilak. Quenna suddenly felt elated and strong. She had come so far and was now returning the Tupilak to its rightful place.

Quenna had brought with her the small pick and the hammer. She knew she must dig down deep to hide the Tupilak to prevent anyone seeing it through the ice.

As she padded through the corridors of white she suddenly caught a fleeting glimpse of a shadow. It reached up to the top of the ice tower and then was gone. Quenna thought she heard distant voices murmuring, but when she looked around, no-one was there.

She sensed she could still be in danger and hurried through the towers of ice, out to the other side where she had rested the dogs.

It looked different to her.

Perhaps, she thought, time and the storms had changed its appearance.

Her footsteps quickened. Then she heard the howl of a dog. She stopped in her tracks and looked around. Still there was no-one and nothing to be seen.

Theo's warm brown eyes came into her mind. 'No, not now,' she said, suddenly engulfed in fear, 'not now.'

Were these sounds ghosts from the past?

Quenna shuddered in horror. Everything around her took on a strangeness. She felt alone and desperate.

Quenna ran, her feet gliding over the ice. She was racing the spirits of time in her search for the site of her discovery. Her eyes glimpsed a dark blue patch marked out on the ice. Yes, the blue ice, that was where she must have chipped out the Tupilak.

Quenna hurried over to the area and fell to her knees. Urgently she began to cut away the darkened icy patch. As she chipped ferociously at the small section, the ice beneath her seemed to move; it felt odd, as if it were swaying.

Then she heard it again, a voice calling out.

This time it was clear, succinct. It was a woman's voice echoing through the ice chambers. 'Stop!' cried the voice. 'Stop, stop, stop!' It echoed desperately out to Quenna.

Quenna placed the Tupilak on the centre of her chipped square. Tap, tap, went the chisel, as she quickly worked on the coloured patch.

'Time to go back,' she said breathlessly to the Tupilak. 'This is where our journey together ends.'

Quenna felt the ice below her shifting sharply. Her heart stopped. Something was wrong. Frightened, she hit at the ice hard with her small hammer, desperate for it all to end, for the Tupilak to be gone.

The small ice block suddenly fell away from her, carrying the Tupilak downwards and out of her sight.

Where was the Tupilak going?

Confused, she looked down into the hole she had made and froze in terror. She was looking straight down into water! It was lapping and bubbling up beneath her body. She saw the Tupilak disappear into the shadowy, murky dark waters just as a woman's voice cried out, 'No!'

Quenna froze in fear. Was it the spirit of the Tupilak crying out as she cast it away?

Reality hit Quenna a second too late. She was floating above deathly cold, deep water. She tried to stand up and jump away, but the ice beneath her jolted and juddered sharply. She fell back onto her knees.

Quenna screamed out. The Tupilak was trying to take her with it!

All around her the ice cracked and splintered. She watched in terror as black veins of torn ice bled out from under her as it wrenched itself apart.

She felt herself falling. Down, down she crashed, helplessly following in the path of the Tupilak. She would join it in the depths and remain in its power forever.

The shattered ice chunks hit the water moments before Quenna. She heard them crunching and splashing into the water.

Then her body went under.

She sank down into freezing darkness and was overwhelmed by the sudden surge of cold.

A terrible pain seared through her body, burning the ice deep into her heart. Her clothes grew heavy and the pain was becoming too much to bear.

Down in the depths Quenna suddenly realised how foolish she had been. Her father had shown her the dangers of blue ice patches. Why hadn't she seen it?

'Quenna, search through the blue and you will find the hidden water,' he had so often told her.

She had chosen that patch because it was blue, foolishly thinking it was where she had dug out the Tupilak. What had happened to her wisdom?

Quenna knew then that she had become so overwhelmed by her grandmother's fear of the Tupilak that she had become blind to the dangers of the real world. Her fear and wild imaginings had finally brought her here, to her death.

She, Quenna, an Inupiaq child, had not read the ice. Pain turned to numbness.

'Beware the cold, Quenna,' her father had told her. 'When you feel nothing, the cold has you beaten.'

The cold was destroying her, with every whisper of her father's words: 'Numbness, death, numbness.'

Then something strange happened. Something drew itself around her. She became veiled in a hard, crisp, black web. Its woven threads drew her body tightly into its clutches. It pierced and dug into her frozen cheeks.

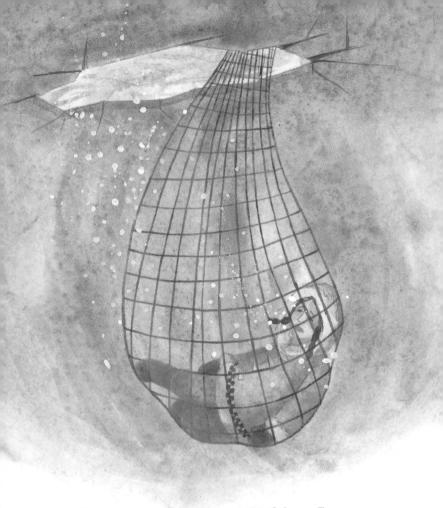

Quenna reached out and her fingers
became locked in the coils of the web. She
felt her body being drawn slowly upwards.
She was rising higher and higher out of the
depths. She tried to move but her limbs
were numb, invisible, gone.

Inch by inch the bottom of the ice floor
above Quenna drew closer, until suddenly

she hit the harsh, cold air. She felt the weight of her wet and heavy body being dragged out of the water.

But it was strange. Quenna felt as if she were somebody else. Something was happening to her; someone was there next to her, yet she saw herself as if she were a distant spectator of her own fate.

Her head became supported by large, warm hands that wrapped tightly around her.

Weak and defeated, Quenna looked up into the face of a woman. The woman was talking to her, but her voice was so far away that Quenna couldn't hear her.

Quenna felt her body being lifted carefully and placed on something solid yet soft. She was flying through the air.

Quenna thought she must be dying and was being carried away by the gods. She closed her eyes and darkness drew in.

When Quenna opened her eyes she saw the tall towers of the ice palace reaching up to the sky. A woman leaned over her and touched her forehead gently, concerned.

Quenna sensed her comfort and smiled feebly into her warm eyes.

It took a moment for Quenna to realise.
Her mind was suddenly overwhelmed
with happiness, because standing before her
was her ice goddess.

CHAPTER NINE
NATURE'S DAUGHTER

The ice goddess had saved her life – or had she? Quenna could see all around her but she couldn't feel her limbs. Was it only her spirit, bodiless, that looked out into the world? Had she joined the ghosts of the Tupilak? How long had she been in the ice palace?

Every time she opened her eyes the sky reflected a different image. Time passed, and as Quenna rested, feeling slowly eked its way back into her invisible limbs.

A strange feeling of comfort seeped into her body as it tingled back to life. At times, in the silence around her, Quenna heard only her own breathing.

Somebody touched Quenna's brow. She looked up into the gentle face of the goddess.

The goddess smiled and raised Quenna's head up to her. She placed a spoon into Quenna's mouth and Quenna felt hot, fishy broth trickle down her throat and warm her insides. It was then that Quenna knew she was alive. She could smell the food and taste its deliciousness.

She looked down. She was covered in furs; polar bear furs, caribou skins and fox enveloped her.

A small fire burned brightly close to where she lay.

The goddess touched Quenna's cheek. 'Ahh, your skin is warm now. I am so happy, I thought we had lost you and we would never get you back,' she said, gently lifting Quenna so that she sat up.

Quenna looked around and suddenly everything came into focus.

Near the entrance to the ice palace a man was standing throwing seal meat to a pack of huskies. He wore traditional hunting skins.

The huskies yelped hungrily at him but sat obediently waiting until the seal pieces were thrown down. Rifles and spears were stacked against the palace walls.

Close to her bed and the fire were two other beds of bear skins, and the objects of a camp were scattered across the ground: tin cups, can openers and a large butane gas cylinder. These brought Quenna back into the real world with a jolt.

The goddess called to the man and he came over. As he drew closer, his weathered skin creased into a big grin. He held up a big, black, heavy fishing net, then dropped it and looked up at the sky in disbelief.

The goddess put her arm around Quenna's shoulder. 'My husband thinks it funny that he set his nets for a walrus and caught a child instead,' she laughed. 'He has many hunting stories to tell his friends, but this one will be the best of all.'

'Is he a god too?' Quenna whispered. Her throat felt raw and her head was fragile.

The goddess laughed and wagged her finger at the man. 'He may be a good hunter, but a god? No. He is only a man, but a very good-hearted man,' she said, winking at him.

The man smiled, then walked back over to the huskies.

Quenna was lost for words.

'You are a lucky child,' continued the goddess. 'You should have died, but you must have been granted good fortune, because we came to check our nets just in time to save you. Didn't you hear me calling you?'

Quenna's mind drifted back to the moment before the fall. Yes, Quenna had thought she had heard the voice of a woman, but she had believed it was the spirit of the Tupilak.

The old woman sighed. 'I was shouting to warn you of Qisuk's fishing holes and what did you do?' she said in exasperation. 'You ran straight into one.' She hugged Quenna affectionately.

'I thought you were the goddess,' Quenna said weakly.

Her words brought a smile and a look of utter delight to the woman's face. 'Oh, how I wish I was! But ahh, I am just a woman, and an old one at that,' she said, chuckling. 'My name is Mikisuk and my husband is called Qisuk.'

Quenna felt a pang of disappointment mingled with relief. 'Oh, Mikisuk,' she said vacantly.

'You can call me the goddess if you like,' Mikisuk said jokingly. 'Perhaps then Qisuk would treat me like one,' she chuckled.

Quenna smiled at her.

Mikisuk got back up and padded across to the primus stove. She ladled some more fish broth into a small cup and took it back to Quenna.

'Qisuk is one of the greatest hunters. That is why you are alive. There is very little that escapes my husband, and you were not going to be the exception,' she said, waving proudly over at him.

Mikisuk handed Quenna the cup of broth. She drank it down and felt warm inside.

Quenna realised that Mikisuk was not a goddess, but her broth tasted like the most magical, healing potion.

Slowly, Quenna was beginning to come back down to earth, to reality.

'You have come far from your village,' Mikisuk said, pointing out of the ice palace back along the pipeline.

'Yes,' Quenna said, puzzled that the woman should know where she had come from.

'Qisuk saw your tracks for some distance,' Mikisuk explained. 'We know your village. We have been through it many times. Qisuk used to visit at the time of the race.'

Of course, the race; Quenna suddenly remembered her father and the accident.

'Mmm, it has been a bad year,' Mikisuk continued. 'There has been a lot of falling ice. All over the area we have heard of accidents. Qisuk felt that this year he would not race, so we did not come to your village or perhaps we would have met you earlier.'

Relief swept through Quenna.

So that was it, she thought, her father's misfortune was not the dark magical forces of the Tupilak but a change in weather conditions. Her father must have hit a fallen ice wall.

'What is your name?' said Mikisuk.

'Quenna.'

'Ah, Quenna, and when you dived into Qisuk's nets were you searching for this?' Mikisuk drew the Tupilak from her pocket and held it out to Quenna.

Quenna gasped in shock and disbelief at the ivory figure in Mikisuk's hand. How could it still be there? She had watched it drop into the depths of the ocean. Quenna felt sick with shock and disappointment. She had failed to end the curse.

Mikisuk sat patiently, waiting for Quenna to take the Tupilak back.

Quenna reached up but couldn't bring herself to touch it. Her hand froze in mid-air as if locked in time. She just gazed at it in fear.

Mikisuk looked intently at Quenna. 'It is a Tupilak,' Mikisuk said calmly. 'I have seen only a few of these over my many years.'

'It is evil,' Quenna said, suddenly tearful. 'Please, I … I can't take it back.'

Mikisuk sighed and looked into the flames of the fire. 'I have heard a Tupilak can hold great power. But I also know of some who have overcome the darkness.' Mikisuk looked questioningly at Quenna.

Quenna looked into the old woman's eyes; they were kind and full of wisdom.

'Do you not now possess a stronger magic?' Mikisuk said. 'Have you not won?' A broad grin drew across Mikisuk's face. 'Can't you see there is no longer anything to fear?'

Quenna looked at the ivory figure.

Mikisuk smiled reassuringly at her. 'See the Tupilak as it really is,' Mikisuk said softly.

Quenna looked closely at it. Yes, Quenna thought, something was different. Something had changed. The carved lines were exactly as they always had been, but it no longer looked the same.

Mikisuk smiled at Quenna and placed the Tupilak in Quenna's hand, gently cupping her fingers over it.

For the first time since discovering the Tupilak, Quenna was losing her fear. She had become a survivor, and her survival was casting away all the terrifying myths and fears of the Tupilak.

Quenna slowly opened up her hand and looked at the carving. Its shape felt familiar to her, comfortable in her palm.

'Now it is your lucky charm,' Mikisuk stated confidently. 'If we had been but a second later or decided to check the other traps before yours, you would have died.' Mikisuk visibly shuddered at the thought.

'Yes,' Quenna said, suddenly smiling down at the Tupilak. 'I have been lucky, haven't I.'

She began to feel a warm glow inside. 'I'm alive.'

'Alive yes, lucky perhaps,' Mikisuk tutted, disapprovingly, 'but foolish, very foolish to wander onto the blue ice. You should not have done it,' she said sternly.

'I'm sorry,' Quenna said, looking across at Qisuk's torn nets.

'Ah, nets are nothing, but survival is everything. You are a child of nature, you must read nature's signs and never ignore them,' Mikisuk said.

'Yes, I am, normally,' Quenna said, 'but I have been on a long journey and ... I made it to the ice palace, didn't I?' Quenna looked up at Mikisuk in triumph.

Mikisuk nodded, smiling. 'Yes, Quenna, you made it. Magic comes in many forms,' Mikisuk said, looking up at the beautiful towering ice walls.

CHAPTER TEN
A NEW BEGINNING

The journey home was the happiest day of Quenna's life.

Qisuk led the way in the first husky train which carried their supplies.

Following on in the second sled, Mikisuk stood behind and Quenna lay wrapped up warm and comfortable in beautiful furs.

Quenna was holding the Tupilak in her hand.

She was alive and the world looked beautiful. She felt as if she was reaching the end of a long journey that had started from the first moment she discovered the Tupilak.

Quenna looked at the Tupilak confidently, knowing that it held no evil. Perhaps it was magic, but now Quenna thought it was something far more precious and powerful than any magic.

It was history. It had come from another time, carrying forward the superstitions and fears of Quenna's people from generations before her, through the eyes of her fragile grandmother.

Someone had lovingly carved the beautiful ivory image, and Quenna suddenly felt that it was special and that she was meant to have it. It was a gift from the past.

Quenna was no longer frightened of the past. Now she looked to the future.

When they arrived at Quenna's home in the village, Mikisuk and Qisuk were treated like the god and goddess Quenna had first believed them to be.

Quenna's parents had spent many heartbreaking days searching the wilderness for her, and the thought that they would never see her again had driven them to despair.

Quenna's grandmother's face melted into happiness, and she gave Quenna a mighty hug that no polar bear could have matched.

After Quenna had been home for a while, it didn't take long for things to return to normal at school and at home. Although Quenna did learn that during her journey to the ice palace there had been some surprising changes.

Her grandmother had actually ventured

out with Ituku and ridden on his bright,
noisy, popping skidoo, searching the area
for her.

Her grandmother now often went out with Ituku, hurtling through the village to socialise with old friends. The thought of this sight had Quenna in stitches.

Also, one night as Quenna sat in her room, Saufak crept in. She saw Quenna holding the Tupilak. 'Does your grandmother know you still have the Tupilak?' her mother said quietly, in the darkness.

Quenna looked up at her and shook her head. 'I've decided not to tell her. She may get frightened again and I don't want her to. It's my secret,' she whispered softly.

Her mother tiptoed over and sat beside her. 'Your grandmother is from another generation. I am so happy that you understand, because I do too now,' her mother said proudly.

'It's so small, isn't it,' Quenna said, holding the Tupilak up in the moonlight.

'Yes, but what an impact that tiny carving has had on us all,' said her mother solemnly.

'Magic?' Quenna asked, smiling.

'Who knows?' Saufak replied wistfully.

Over the weeks a calm returned to Quenna's home. Saufak often sat with Quenna and her mother, frantically stitching the new mittens and kamiks, eager to help replace the stock lost in the fire. Quenna's grandmother's face was full of pride.

The Tupilak had changed everyone.

As time went on, Quenna's father's crutches became less and less necessary and Saufak no longer had to frog-march Quenna to the community centre to use the computers.

This Quenna did for herself.

Every evening after school she ran to the centre and used the computer to write a story.

This story.

The story about the beautiful Tupilak.

Glossary

Ajarraaq
A string puzzle game used like a cat's cradle.
The puzzles can be quite complicated and
are often used to tell stories or rhymes.

Originally strips of sealskin were used,
but today it is generally string.

Inupiaq
Inupiaq is one group of the Inuit peoples
living mainly around the shores of Alaska,
Canada and Greenland.

Another Inuit group is called the Yupik
and they live in Siberia and western Alaska.

Kamiks
Traditional hand-stitched boots made from
sealskin or other skins and stitched with
ivaluq (narwhal sinews).

Skins are still used and stitched in
the traditional way, but instead of using
traditional ivaluq, craftsmen today use
dental floss as thread because it is stronger
and more convenient.

Kayak
A traditional Inuit boat that was originally made to measure for each individual so that they sat neatly tucked under waterproof, stitched skins pulled tightly over a frame.

Musher
Sled drivers.

Nanuq
The Inuktitut word for polar bear.

Piklirtautiniq
A game where children jump as quickly as they can from a kneeling position onto their feet.

Qulittaq
A caribou-skin parka with a fur-trimmed hood.

Tupilak
A figure carved from ivory or soapstone, often made in secret and thought to carry much magic. The strange-looking carvings were believed to become real monsters and destroy their victims unless a stronger magic turned the carving against its original maker.